PEBBLES AND BAMM-BAMM
THE NEW KID ON THE BLOCK

Story by Horace J. Elias

Published by Ottenheimer Publishers, Inc.

Copyright © Hanna-Barbera Productions, Inc., 1975, 1986

Printed in Brazil

Fred Flintstone came home one day from his
job at the rock mine. As usual, he slammed the
front door so hard the whole house shook, a piece

of the roof dropped off, dishes fell off the shelves, and all the dogs on the street started to howl.

"WILMA! I'M HOME!" he bellowed.

"That's nice, dear," called Wilma from the kitchen. "Dinner will be ready in a minute, as

soon as I pick up the dishes!"

After dinner, Fred remembered something.
"Say, Wilma," he said, "we have a new guy at the

rock mine. He's an expert at speeding things up and making them run better. He's supposed to show us how to dig more rock faster, and stuff like that. And he's just moved his family into a house up the street. They have a baby about Pebbles'

age, and I told him he could bring the kid down here tomorrow to play with Pebbles and Bamm-Bamm. Okay?"

"Certainly, dear," said Wilma.

In the middle of the morning of the next day, a pleasant-looking lady walked into the Flintstones' front yard, where Pebbles and Bamm-Bamm were playing quietly. Wilma stepped out of the front door and the lady said,

"I'm Mrs. Bonaparte, and this is my little boy Stonewell. He's Stonewell Bonaparte III, but we call him Stoney Boney, because that's all he ever says!"

"My goodness!" cried Wilma. "That's a coincidence! The redhead is my daughter Pebbles—

and all SHE ever says is 'Da Da Goo Goo'! The little blond boy is Bamm-Bamm—and all HE ever says is his name!"

"Well," said Mrs. Bonaparte, "I'm sure they'll get along just fine. I've got to run along now. I'll pick Stoney Boney up at lunch time."

Before we get into what happened next, we'd better understand something. It's quite true that all Pebbles ever said was "Da Da Goo Goo" and all

Bamm-Bamm ever said was his name. But depending on how they said it, it could mean a lot of different things. And as we know, the same was true of Stonewell Bonaparte III. So to save time, we'll say what they MEANT instead of what they SAID. All clear? Here's what happened:

Pebbles and Bamm-Bamm were making mud pies. They stopped to say "hello" to Stoney Boney. He looked at what they were doing and said, "That's no way to make mud pies! You need lots more mud and a lot more water!"

Pebbles and Bamm-Bamm looked at each other. Then Bamm-Bamm said, "This is the way we always make mud pies. We like them this way."

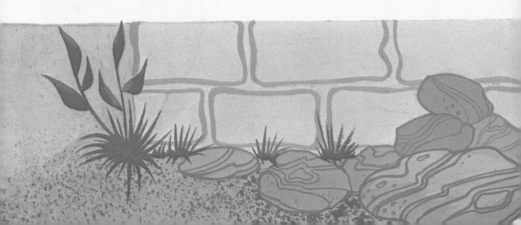

Stoney Boney said, "What a pair of ninnies! Don't you know ANYTHING? Why don't you play faster? Think of how much better it would be—you'd get a lot more playing done!"

Pebbles said, "We're not trying to get ANYTHING done—we're just PLAYING!"

"Look!" said Stoney Boney. "Let me show you!" And he began to pick up things and move them someplace else. Then he very rapidly built a

pile of stones. Then he took a stick and dug a hole.
   Bamm-Bamm looked at all the things Stoney
Boney had moved around. He looked at the pile of
stones and the hole. Then he said, "Stoney Boney,

why don't you just relax?"

"Well!" said Stoney Boney. "I can see you two need some teaching. Now. I've got a great game to play. Are you ready?"

"What's the name of the game?" asked Pebbles.

"It's called 'War'," answered Stoney Boney.

"I don't like the name," said Pebbles. "It sounds terrible. How do you play it?"

"Listen!" cried Stoney Boney. "First, you take something that belongs to me. Then I yell at you. Then you yell at me. Then I hit you, and then we fight. Ready?"

"Bamm-Bamm," said Pebbles, "I think we've got a crazy one here."

"What's the matter?" cried Stoney Boney. "You scared or something?"

"I don't know what that means," said Pebbles. "First of all, we don't take things that belong to other people. Second, if you took something that belonged to me, I'd guess that you borrowed it and would give it back when you were finished with it."

"And besides," added Bamm-Bamm, "we don't like to do things in a big hurry just to be doing it fast. We like to play the way we like to play!"

Stoney Boney snorted, "I can see you're nothing but a couple of BABIES—you don't want to DO anything!"

"Right," said Pebbles. "Time enough for that when we grow up."

And Bamm-Bamm said, "We're not even in a
hurry to do THAT! The way I hear the grown-ups
carrying on, yelling and fighting, I'm gonna stay

the way I am for as long as I can!"
When Mrs. Bonaparte had called for Stoney

Boney and taken him home for lunch, Bamm-Bamm said to Pebbles, "Think he'll be back?"

"No way," answered Pebbles. "He's too dog-gone CIVILIZED for us!"